HANDTALK
SCHOOL

MARY BETH MILLER & GEORGE ANCONA

Four Winds Press   New York

Collier Macmillan Canada   Toronto

Maxwell Macmillan International Publishing Group
New York   Oxford   Singapore   Sydney

COME   VISIT   MY   SCHOOL.

Library of Congress Cataloging-in-Publication Data   Mary Beth. Handtalk school / Mary Beth Miller & George Ancona.   p.   cm. Summary: Words and sign language depict a group of students involved in putting on a Thanksgiving play at a school for deaf children. ISBN 0-02-700912-2. 1. Sign language—Juvenile literature. 2. Children, Deaf—United States—Juvenile literature. [1. Sign language. 2. Deaf.] I. Ancona, George. II. Title. HV2476.M37   1991   419—dc20   90-24030

This book is dedicated to our friend Debbie Matthews, who inspired us to do this book.

Thanks to all those who participated in this book. *The adults:* Judith Bravin, Joan Dochtermann, Barbara Kannapell, Naomi Leeds, and George Martens. *The children:* Roxanne Aguilo, Ramon Feliciano, Tara Giambalvo, Shira Grabelsky (and Jeff and Karen, her parents), Tonia Jackson, Johnnie Ma, Richard Pinkert, Corey Porte, Shelina Reneau, Jen Soumvilaysack, Janell Wagstaff, and Jeffrey Young. Thanks also to Sister Bernadette Downes, and to our sign-language interpreters, Debbie Matthews and Marie Taccogna.

MEET MY CLASS!

JEFF

JANELL

JOHNNIE MA

THEIR NAMES ARE

TARA

SHIRA JEN

GET UP!

JEN . . .

TODAY'S

OUR

PLAY.

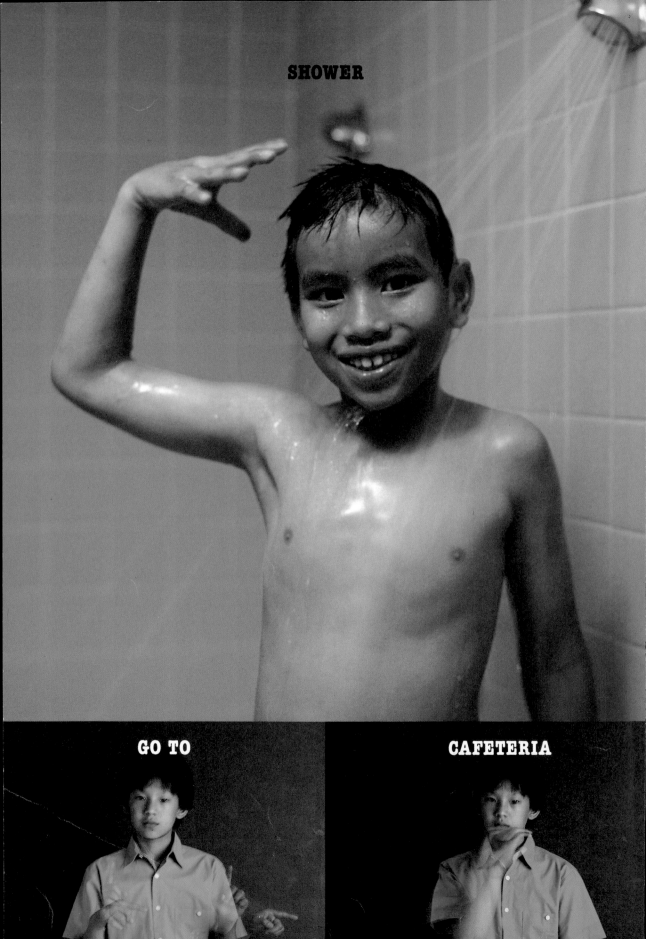

SHOWER

GO TO

CAFETERIA

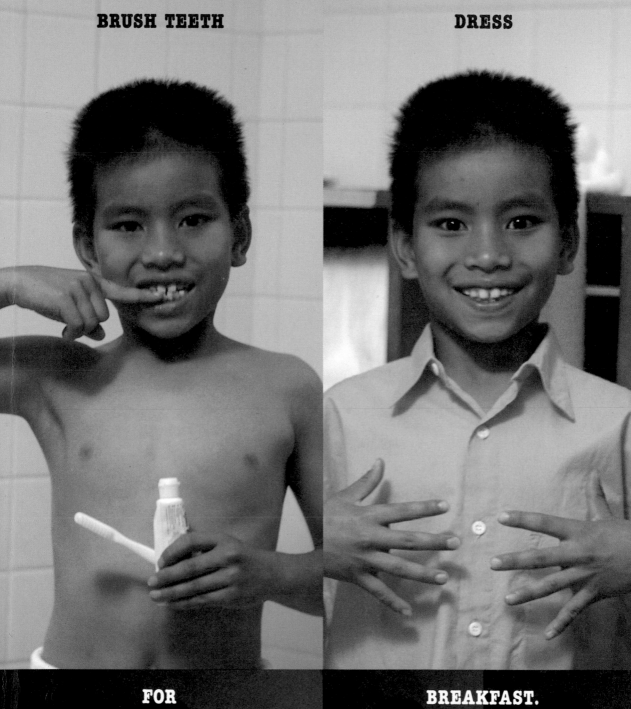

BRUSH TEETH

DRESS

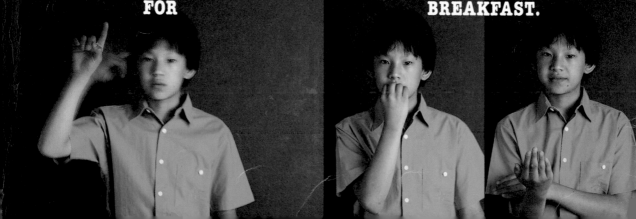

FOR

BREAKFAST.

JUICE

CEREAL

MILK

MUFFIN

EGGS

BANANA

GOOD   MORNING!

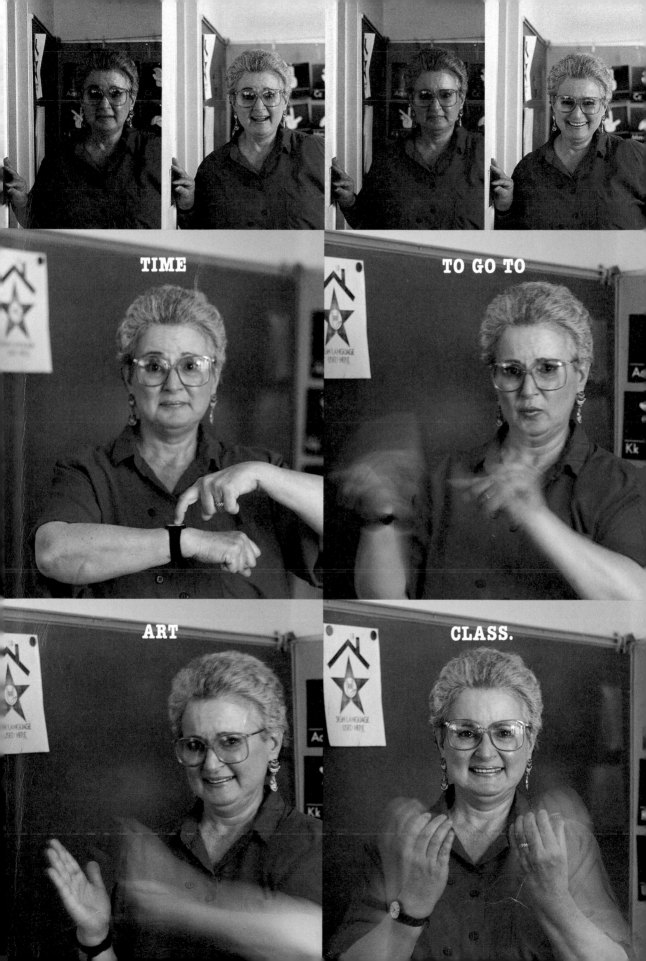

TIME

TO GO TO

ART

CLASS.

ADD **SUBTRACT**

MATH **CLASS**

SIGNS STORIES.

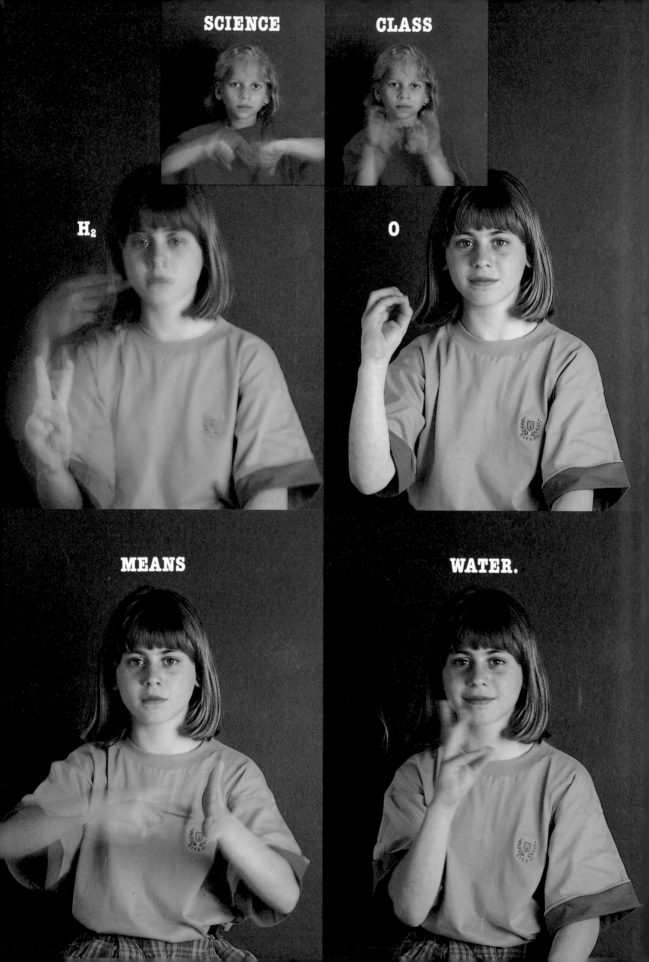

SCIENCE CLASS H_2 O MEANS WATER.

Native American:

Welcome !

Pilgrim:

Let's Celebrate !

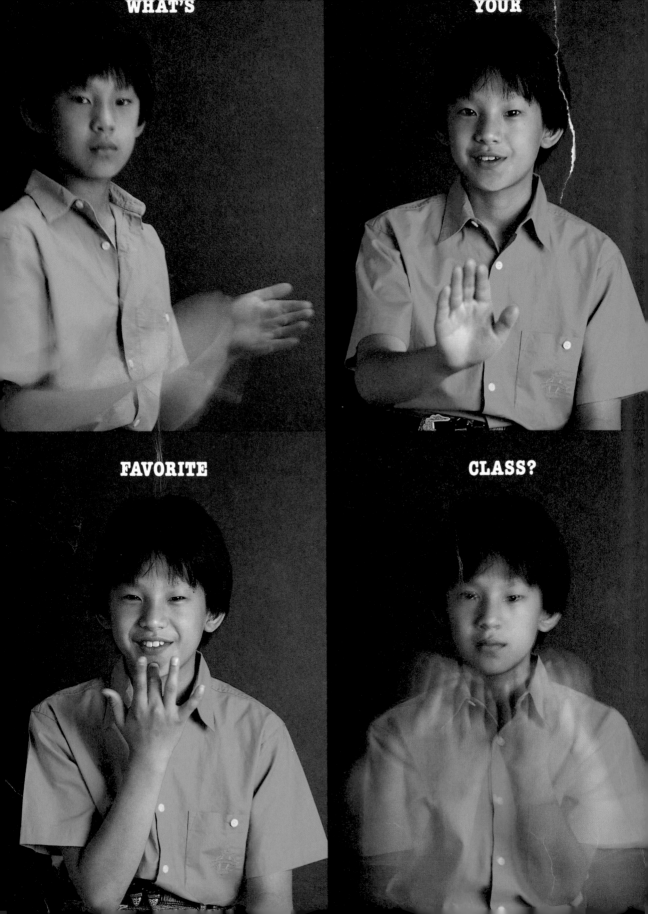

WRESTLING VOLLEYBALL BASKETBALL

TRACK   SOCCER   CHEERLEADING

DAD CAN COME.

WELCOME TO OUR

THANKSGIVING PLAY.

NOW WE CAN GO

HOME FOR THANKSGIVING!

Residential Schools for the Deaf

ALABAMA: Alabama School for the Deaf, Talladega

ARIZONA: Arizona State School for the Deaf, Tucson

ARKANSAS: Arkansas School for the Deaf, Little Rock

CALIFORNIA: California School for the Deaf, Fremont; California School for the Deaf, Riverside

COLORADO: Colorado School for the Deaf, Colorado Springs

CONNECTICUT: American School for the Deaf, West Hartford

DELAWARE: Margaret S. Sterek School for the Hearing Impaired, Newark

DISTRICT OF COLUMBIA: Kendall Demonstration Elementary School; Model Secondary School for the Deaf

FLORIDA: Florida School for the Deaf, St. Augustine

GEORGIA: Georgia School for the Deaf, Cave Spring

HAWAII: Hawaii School for the Deaf, Honolulu

IDAHO: Idaho School for the Deaf, Gooding

ILLINOIS: Illinois School for the Deaf, Jacksonville

INDIANA: Indiana School for the Deaf, Indianapolis

IOWA: Iowa School for the Deaf, Council Bluffs

KANSAS: Kansas School for the Deaf, Olathe

KENTUCKY: Kentucky School for the Deaf, Danville

LOUISIANA: Louisiana School for the Deaf, Baton Rouge

MAINE: Governor Baxter School for the Deaf, Portland

MARYLAND: Maryland School for the Deaf, Frederick & Columbia

MASSACHUSETTS: Beverly School for the Deaf, Beverly; Boston School for the Deaf, Randolph; The Learning Center for Deaf Children, Framingham

MICHIGAN: Michigan School for the Deaf, Flint; Lutheran School for the Deaf, Detroit

MINNESOTA: Minnesota State Academy for the Deaf, Faribault

MISSISSIPPI: Mississippi School for the Deaf, Jackson

MISSOURI: Missouri School for the Deaf, Fulton

MONTANA: Montana School for the Deaf, Great Falls

NEBRASKA: Nebraska School for the Deaf, Omaha

NEW JERSEY: Marie H. Katzenbach School for the Deaf, West Trenton

NEW MEXICO: New Mexico School for the Deaf, Santa Fe

NEW YORK: New York School for the Deaf, White Plains; New York State School for the Deaf, Rome; Rochester School for the Deaf, Rochester; St. Mary's School for the Deaf, Buffalo

NORTH CAROLINA: North Carolina School for the Deaf, Morganton

NORTH DAKOTA: North Dakota School for the Deaf, Devils Lake

OHIO: Ohio State School for the Deaf, Columbus; St. Rita School for the Deaf, Cincinnati

OKLAHOMA: Oklahoma School for the Deaf, Sulphur

OREGON: Oregon School for the Deaf, Salem

PENNSYLVANIA: Scranton State School for the Deaf, Scranton; The Pennsylvania School for the Deaf, Philadelphia; Western Pennsylvania School for the Deaf, Edgewood

RHODE ISLAND: Rhode Island School for the Deaf, Providence

SOUTH CAROLINA: South Carolina School for the Deaf, Spartanburg

SOUTH DAKOTA: South Dakota School for the Deaf, Sioux Falls

TENNESSEE: Tennessee School for the Deaf, Knoxville

TEXAS: Texas School for the Deaf, Austin

UTAH: Utah School for the Deaf, Ogden

VERMONT: Augustine School for the Deaf, Brattleboro

VIRGINIA: Virginia State School for the Deaf at Hampton, Hampton; Virginia School for the Deaf, Staunton

WASHINGTON: Washington State School for the Deaf, Vancouver

WEST VIRGINIA: West Virginia School for the Deaf, Romney

WISCONSIN: St. John's School for the Deaf, Milwaukee; Wisconsin School for the Deaf, Delavan

WYOMING: Wyoming School for the Deaf, Casper

Geography lesson: find these cities on your map!